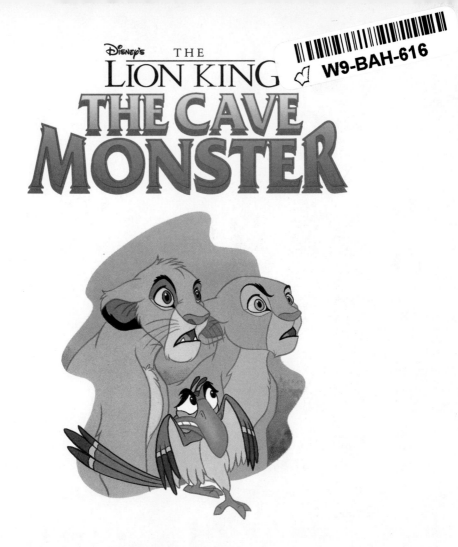

DISNEY'S THE LION KING
THE CAVE MONSTER

By Justine Korman
Illustrated by Don Williams

A GOLDEN BOOK • NEW YORK
Golden Books Publishing Company, Inc., Racine, Wisconsin 53404

One day Simba and Nala went for a ramble in the forest. Zazu flew overhead to keep an eye on the curious cubs.

Soon the young lions came upon a dark cave they had never seen before.

"Let's see what's inside!" Nala exclaimed.
"Be careful, you two," Zazu urged.
But, of course, neither cub listened to the cautious bird.

Simba pushed his way in front of Nala. "I should look first, since I'm going to be the Lion King." "But you aren't as brave as I am," Nala replied. "I'm braver!" Simba declared.

The two cubs wrestled as they argued over who was the braver.

Nala said, "I'm not scared of you!"

"I'm not scared of anything!" bragged Simba.

With that, Nala flipped Simba over her shoulder.

He landed with a plop just outside the cave.

Before Zazu could stop him, Simba scrambled
to his feet and stuck his head into the dark, dark cave.

Two eyes shone from the back of the cave. A deep, scary voice demanded, "Who dares to disturb me?"

The voice echoed like thunder. Simba tried to make himself sound fearless as he answered, "It is I, Simba, the future Lion King."

"And I am Anansi, ruler of the forest!" the deep
voice rumbled in reply. "I'm as big as the sky and
as fierce as a storm. And I eat twenty elephants for
breakfast!"

When Zazu heard that, his feathers shook with fright. "A monster!" he said, trembling. "I'll summon the king!" And away he flapped.

The deep voice laughed. "King Mufasa, ha! I'll tie a knot in his tail."

"You wouldn't dare!" Simba said.

The answer was an echoing ROAR that seemed to shake the whole forest. Simba shuddered. What monster was so powerful that it did not fear the great Lion King?

"I think I'm scared now," Simba whispered.
Nala looked at the dark mouth of the cave. "Well,
I'm not scared of a monster if I haven't seen it with
my own eyes," she said.

Nala crept into the inky darkness. Simba watched until he couldn't see even the tip of Nala's tail. Suddenly he heard a very loud scream!

Simba raced into the narrow cave to save his friend. He saw Nala pressed against the wall. She pointed to the blackness at the back of the cave.

"I guess I *am* afraid of something," Nala whimpered. To the lion cubs' surprise, Nala sounded like a monster herself when her voice echoed loudly in the cave.

Just then a creature stepped into the light. In front of Simba stood a tiny spider.

"Are you the monster?" asked Simba in amazement.

"Anansi," the spider said meekly. "I was only trying to defend myself. You don't know how scary it is to be small."

Simba laughed in relief.

Then the cubs heard a mighty, terrifying ROAR!
"That must be my father," Simba said.

Sure enough, Mufasa's deep voice called into the cave. "Come out and defend yourself, forest ruler! It is I, the Lion King! I have come to save my son and his best friend."

Nala and Simba trotted out of the cave, but the little spider hung back.

"Don't be afraid," Simba said. "My father won't be angry once we tell him what happened."

But it wasn't the mighty Lion King Anansi feared. "Please don't let that awful bird eat me," the spider begged.

Zazu looked around in alarm. "Awful bird?! What? Where?"

Mufasa stared at the little spider. "This is the forest ruler who eats twenty elephants for breakfast?" he demanded.

Simba looked at Nala and they both burst out laughing.

"Well?" Mufasa prompted.

Simba began the story. "Nala and I were trying to see who was braver," he said.

"But the cave scared Simba," Nala said.
"And then Anansi scared you," Simba added.
"That awful bird still scares me," Anansi piped up.
"Well, very little scares me," Zazu bragged.

"Enough!" Mufasa chuckled, turning to leave. "Long stories scare me."

"It seems everyone is afraid of something," Zazu pointed out, flying up into the sky. "Even the Lion King."